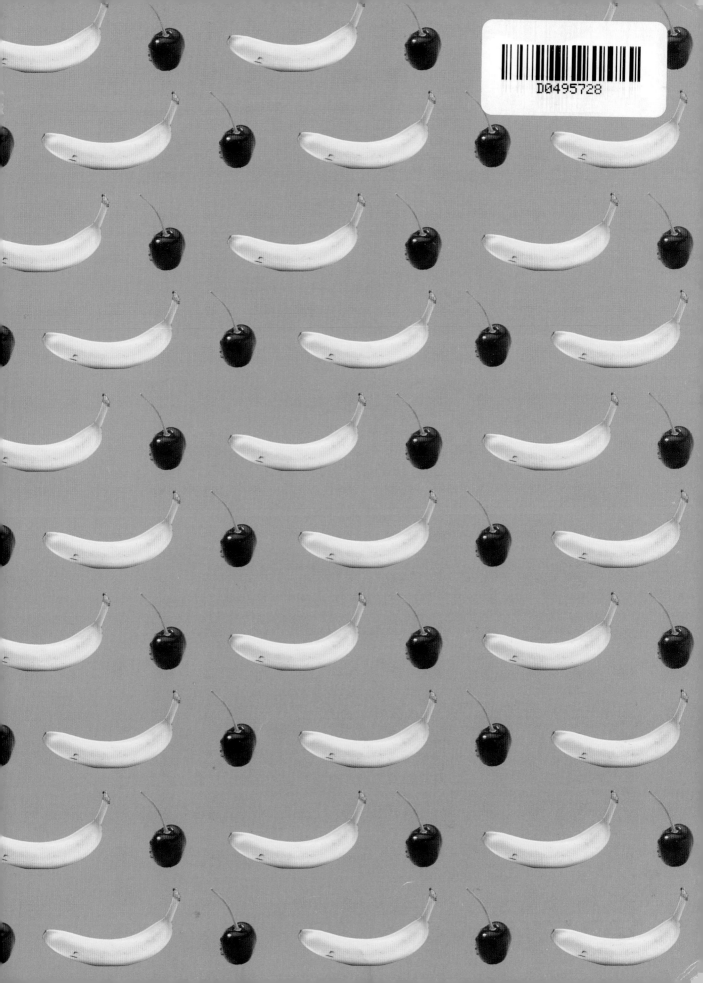

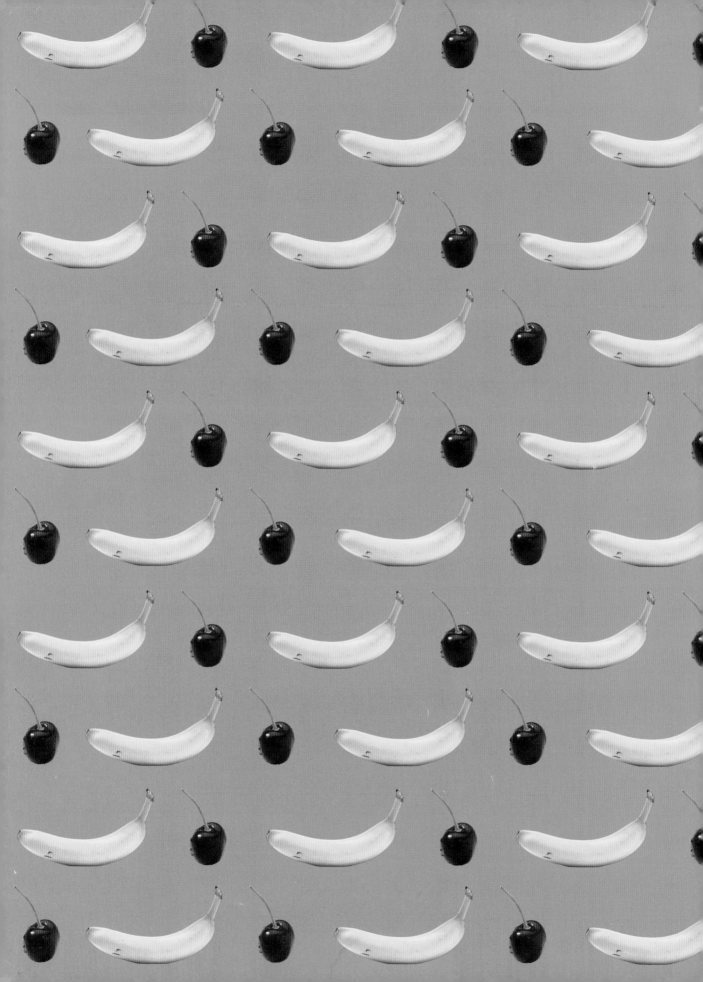

So Hungry

a story by
Daniel Morden

illustrated by
Suzanne Carpenter

P O N T

To the Tregenzas – foodies every one!

D.M.

Heaps of love to the hungry, hungry Breckons.

S.C.

First Impression – 2004
Second Impression – 2006

ISBN 1 84323 368 1

© text: Daniel Morden
© illustrations: Suzanne Carpenter

Printed in Wales at Gomer Press, Llandysul, Ceredigion SA44 4JL

One fine day I went swimming.

And then I drove back

past the Sugar Loaf Mountain

past the Blorenge Mountain

and then HOME!

When I got home,
Dad was out.

It was late and all the shops
were shut.

I was SO HUNGRY!

I went straight to the fridge.
Was there anything to eat in the fridge?

Was there anything to eat in the cupboard?

Was there anything to eat
in the fruit bowl?

NOTHING.
Nothing to eat in the whole house!

I thought, I'll go to sleep.
When you're asleep,
you don't feel hungry.
So I put on my pyjamas.
I jumped into bed.
I shut my eyes.
But I couldn't sleep.

I was SO HUNGRY!
I couldn't stop thinking about food.

At last I fell asleep. I had a dream.
I dreamt I sat in a boat on the sea.
But the boat was a baked potato!

The oars were
made of …

… LEEKS.

The sun was a …
… FRIED EGG.
The sea was
made of …

… BAKED BEANS.

In my dream I came to an island ...

I walked into a forest
and found my car.

Off I went!

I drove past the Sugar Loaf mountain

past the Blorenge mountain

And then I was HOME.
I went inside and there was my Dad.
But he was DIFFERENT! His head was …

a PEACH.

His nose was …

an EGG.

His eyes were …

TOMATOES.

His hair was …

a CABBAGE.

His teeth were ...

PEAS in a POD.

I shook Dad by the hand and one of his fingers came off.

It was DELICIOUS!

I went out of the house and there was a mountain …

... of mashed POTATO!

And then I woke up.

I was eating

... MY QUILT!

When the shops opened we bought all our

FAVOURITE FOOD.   It was so-o lovely.

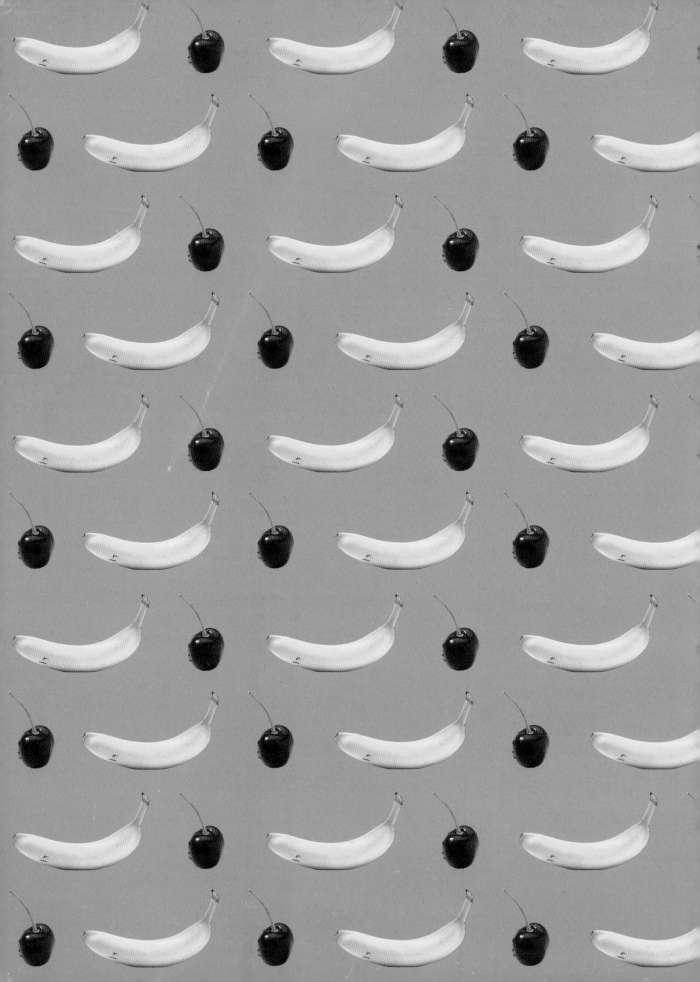